Mickey and Pluto were busy doing chores all day. "Well, Pluto," said Mickey. "I think we've done a good day's work. How about a **little nap**? You've certainly earned it!"

Pluto shook his head and barked, "Woof-woof!" He wanted to stay and help Mickey. There would be no nap for Pluto.

Mickey smiled. "C'mon, boy," he said. "We all have to stop and take a rest when we're feeling **sleepy**."

But Pluto was not convinced. He didn't feel the least bit tired! And to prove it, he ran around the yard three times!

"Okay," said Mickey. "We'll keep going, I guess. Let me get the rake."

Mickey's backyard was covered in **colorful** fall leaves.

When Mickey finished raking, Pluto took a **flying leap** and landed right in the middle of one big pile.

"Now you've done it!" said Mickey. "I'll have to start all over again."

While Mickey raked the leaves again, Pluto brought over three wicker baskets. But by the third basket, the persistent pup started to look a little **sleepy**.

"Pay attention, Pluto," said Mickey. "Watch what you're doing!"

Just then, Pluto yawned a great big yawn. He curled up against the third basket, knocking it over and spilling leaves everywhere. Mickey stood there, shaking his head. "That's what happens when there's **no nap** for Pluto," he said.

"How about that nap, *now*, fella?" asked Mickey. But Pluto felt **wide-awake** again. He shook his head and barked. "All right," said Mickey. "Let's wash the patio."

Pluto **jumped to his feet**. Grabbing the hose with his mouth, he pulled it into place.

"Okay, boy," said Mickey. "I'm turning the water on. Hold that hose steady! Ready? One, two, three. . ."

Just then, Pluto's **sleepy eyes** began to close, and he lost control of the hose! *Whoosh, whizzz, whoops!* Water flew everywhere! Pluto ended up watering the back of the house along with Mickey's freshly washed laundry.

"Oh no!" cried Mickey, shaking his head. "That's what happens when there's no nap for Pluto!"

"Now," said Mickey, "I'll have to wash you and my clothes **all over again**!" He wagged his finger at Pluto. "Don't move! I'm going inside to get the laundry basket!"

But, when Mickey opened the door, his neighbor's cat ran inside.

Mickey didn't see the cat, but Pluto did! Rushing in through his doggy door, Pluto chased after it. He left a trail of muddy paw prints wherever he went. And that was pretty much every room in the house.

"What is all this?" cried Mickey as the cat raced down the stairs. "How did you...what did I...Pluto, stop!" Mickey quickly opened the front door and let the cat out.

Mickey looked around the room. "Gosh!" he said. "This is what happens when there's **no nap** for Pluto. Well, it took two to make this mess. And I guess it will take two to clean it up."

"Here, boy! Here, Pluto!" Mickey called and whistled. But **Pluto didn't come**.

"**Gosh**," said Mickey. "That's funny. Pluto always comes when I call. I guess I'll just have to follow the muddy trail." The paw prints stopped right in front of Mickey's den.

"Aha!" he cried. "Busted!" But when Mickey entered the room, he saw Pluto lying in his cozy bed **fast asleep**.

"Well," said Mickey. "I guess it's **nap time for Pluto** after all. And, like I always say. . .if you can't beat 'em, join 'em!"

So Mickey **curled up** in his big comfy chair, and he was snoring peacefully in no time.